ANGEL WITH A BROKEN WING

Tammy Jensen

authorHOUSE

AuthorHouse™
1663 Liberty Drive, Suite 200
Bloomington, IN 47403
www.authorhouse.com
Phone: 1-800-839-8640

© *2007 Tammy Jensen. All rights reserved.*

No part of this book may be reproduced, stored in a retrieval system, or transmitted by any means without the written permission of the author.

First published by AuthorHouse 11/26/2007

ISBN: 978-1-4343-1509-0 (sc)

Library of Congress Control Number: 2007908671

Printed in the United States of America
Bloomington, Indiana

This book is printed on acid-free paper.

Special thanks from the author to the following people for their support in making the publication of this book possible:

1) Cindy Venable
2) Pam & Danny Rigney
3) Miki DeLane Raines
4) Jay Clarke
5) Kristina & Evan Keese
6) Alaric & Jude Allen
7) Martina Flores
8) Catherine Dole Pedigo
9) Mrs. Min Liu
10) Sarah & John Cobb
11) Mrs. Jennifer Granger Guidry
12) Linda & Howard Carter
13) Candy, Morgan & Mason Huffmaster
14) Scott Jensen
15) Alaric & Jude Allen
16) Kim Menifee and daughter, Charlye Williams

Contents

Chapter One
Little Angels — 1

Chapter Two
Heaven's Gate — 5

Chapter Three
Telling Mom — 11

Chapter Four
The First Visit — 15

Chapter Five
Making Friends — 24

Chapter Six
The Plan — 33

Chapter Seven
An Extra Seat On The Bus — 39

Chapter One

LITTLE ANGELS

"Mom, when we go to heaven will there be lots of little kids there too?" Jenny was only six years old and her best friend's name was Jericho. They did everything together and they would be starting school again next week. They had made all kinds of plans and couldn't wait to get back to school and see their other friends.

"I'm sure there will be many there who were children when they left this world, but I'm not sure what age they'll be in heaven or even if there will be different ages." Jenny sat beside her mother on the bed while her mother wiped the tears from her eyes. She pulled the covers up and tucked them in snugly around Jenny.

"Do the kids in heaven get to play and go to school?" She was trying hard not to cry, but the tears seemed to just keep falling.

"Maybe. But, I think they spend a lot of time looking out for the boys and girls that are still here too." She knew Jenny was worried about Jericho and that somehow Jenny was preparing for the worst.

"If Jericho goes to heaven, will he be looking out for me?" She had a hopeful look in her eye, like they would still be together if only this was true.

"I don't know sweetie, but I believe there is a little angel looking after you right now. I'll bet Jericho even has one looking out for him." Mom was stroking Jenny's hair now. It was blonde and soft and felt like satin.

"Where was Jericho's angel this afternoon Mom?"

"I don't know baby. Bad things happen sometimes and we just have to know that there is a reason. I know this is hard to understand right now, but it's true."

Jenny laid quietly feeling her mom's warm tears on her cheeks and getting some comfort from knowing Mom understood, but when she closed her eyes she'd see Jericho running to chase the ball and the car coming towards him. You could hear the music in the car playing and tires squealing. She tripped and fell trying to run with Jericho. Jericho never saw the car. He was looking back at Jenny and laughing. The boys in the car never saw Jericho. They were shouting and singing.

Jenny dropped to the floor beside her bed and prayed a special prayer for Jericho and his Mom and Dad. She crawled back up into her bed, curled up tight with her doll and began to drift off to sleep.

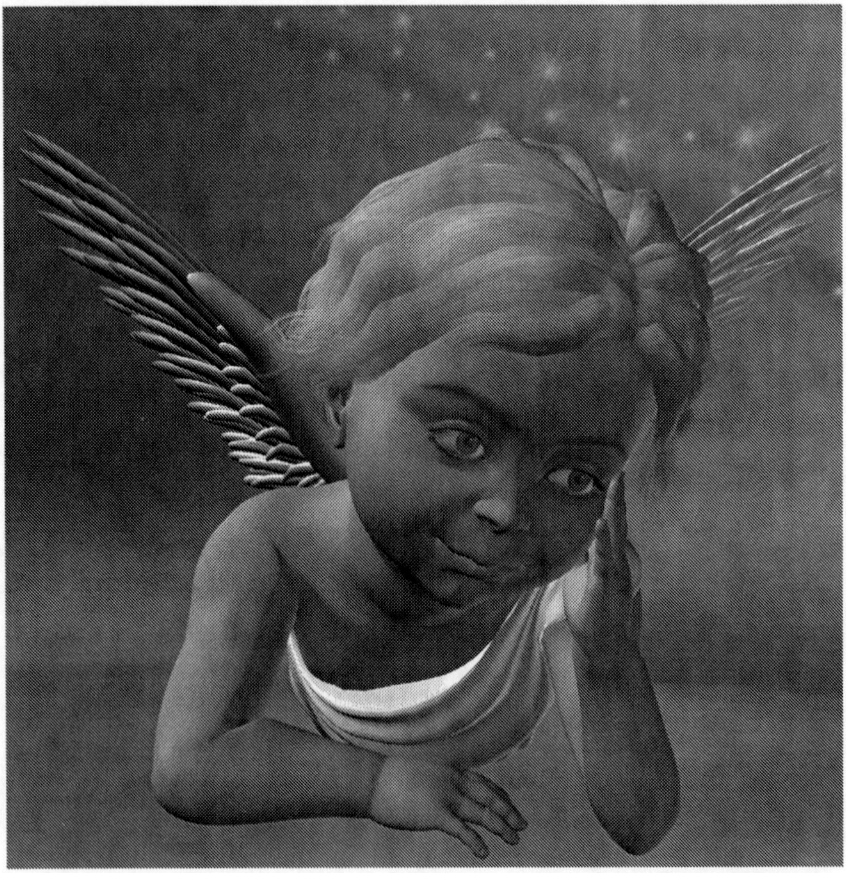

Chapter Two
HEAVEN'S GATE

"Jenny. Jenny. Wake up Jenny." She felt someone touch her softly on the arm. Jenny opened her eyes and there was a cool breeze that drifted across her body. There was the smell of peaches and strawberries and there were thousands of butterflies floating all around. She sat up and looked around and saw groups of children playing and telling stories. These were no ordinary children – they were little angels and one stood right beside her, holding her hand. They weren't at all the way Jenny had imaged angels to be. They were so little. Their little wings were so delicate and worked in and out continuously with slow graceful movements. They were so beautiful she couldn't believe her eyes.

"Where am I?" asked Jenny.

"You're at Heaven's Gate," said the little angel, "This is as far as you can go right now. No one is allowed into heaven before they've passed on."

"But I don't see a gate," exclaimed Jenny.

"It's just a place, not a real gate," stated the angel, "It's kind of like a playground for us little angels when you guys are sleeping or if we're waiting for someone new to look out for."

"Don't <u>you</u> sleep?" asked Jenny.

"Nope, no time for that. We're way to busy."

"Are you my angel?" she asked.

"Nope. I'm Mica. I look out for Jericho," he bragged.

Jenny was shocked. She didn't know what to say. She looked at Mica for a moment and then noticed a bandage on his arm.

"What happened to your arm?" she asked.

"Oh, that. It'll be okay. I just didn't get out of the way in time." He looked down at his arm with pride over the bandage.

"Out of the way of what?"

"The car," he snorted, as if she was supposed to know what he was talking about.

"The car?" She was confused. "What car?" she thought.

"We were watching you play today with Jericho. I saw the car coming and pushed Jericho out of the way, but he hit his head when he fell and I scraped my arm on the car."

"We?" asked Jenny.

"Me and Laurel," stated Mica.

"Who's Laurel?" asked Jenny.

"She's <u>your</u> angel."

Jenny turned and there she was. She was so beautiful and tiny. She walked up to Jenny and took her hand. Jenny just stood and stared.

"I'm sorry I tripped you, but you were gonna get hurt Jenny," said Laurel. "It's not your turn to pass yet."

"Tripped me?" asked Jenny.

"Yeah, this morning when you were running after Jericho. I tripped you before you got to the street so the car wouldn't hit you," said Laurel.

"That was you?"

"Yes." The little angel turned and pointed at another angel, not quite so little as the rest, "See that angel over there? That's Benjamin. He watches out over the boy that was driving the car."

Jenny looked at Benjamin and saw he was crying and there was something wrong with his wing,

"Is his wing broken?" asked Jenny.

"Yes," said Laurel, "The boy that was driving the car had been helped so many times that he just couldn't be helped anymore. Benjamin wanted to give it one more try, but the boy just couldn't hear him. He's not hearing our voices anymore and he's getting to big to be pulled out of harm's way."

"What do you mean?" Jenny asked.

"Well, you know when you're thinking about doing something bad and something tells you not to do it? That's your angel's voice. Sometimes I guess people just get to big to hear their angel's voice or they just don't hear <u>anybody</u> talking to them anymore."

Laurel just looked at Benjamin and sighed, "It's sad when we loose our purpose. God assigns us to a child and it's that child's faith and innocence that makes us strong. When that's gone, we are in danger. That's how Benjamin broke his wing. He'll never fly again unless the boy can hear Benjamin's voice again. That's why you're here."

"Me? What can I do?" asked Jenny.

"He was hurt pretty bad in the accident, but he still has a chance. You have to go back and talk to the boy. You have to teach him to hear Benjamin's voice," begged the little angel.

"How am I supposed to do that?" cried Jenny.

"You can hear my voice when I talk to you, Jenny. I know you do. All you have to do is teach him to truly listen. If not, the boy passes and Benjamin will never fly again."

"Then will the boy come here?" Jenny asked.

"No. He has to hear the voices to pass through here. This is not the destination for boys and girls. They get to go to Heaven. This place is only for little angels. God made us different."

"What will happen to Benjamin?" asked Jenny.

"He'll go on to another purpose, but he'll never fly again and never be given another chance to watch over a child again."

"What about Jericho? Will he be okay?" Jenny asked.

"Sure. He'll be fine," Laurel said, "He just bumped his head. He'll sleep now for a few days, until his head feels better, and then he'll wake up."

Jenny walked over to Benjamin and put her hand on his arm. She felt so sorry for him she almost cried.

"I'm Jenny," she said.

"Yes, I know," said Benjamin, "I'm sorry about your friend, but he'll be okay soon."

"I'm sorry about your wing," said Jenny.

"It doesn't hurt. I just can't fly." Benjamin looked at Jenny and began to smile, "You have a lot of faith Jenny, and God helps us to do whatever we set out to do for Him."

Jenny knew at that very moment that she had to try to help Benjamin. She didn't know how she'd do it, but she had to try. Jericho was going to be okay and these little angels needed her help. God would want her to help. She was very determined to help Benjamin and she smiled just knowing she had been chosen for this special job.

They all began saying goodbye to Jenny and with each little angel's kiss she began to feel more confident. They each hugged Jenny and gave her a special kiss for luck and she began to feel very sleepy. The angels laid her in a golden cloud and she drifted off to sleep.

Chapter Three
TELLING MOM

When Jenny awoke the next morning she smelled bacon and hot chocolate coming from the kitchen. She stretched and yawned and looked out the window. It was a beautiful day. The sun was shining and she could hear the birds singing and playing outside her window. Suddenly, she remembered her dream. Was it a dream? God had sent the little angels to ask for her help. She had to hurry and get started. How was she going to get the boy to hear Benjamin? God knew how. She'd just make sure she was there and somehow she would just know what to do.

She jumped up out of bed, threw on her robe, glided into her slippers, and ran off to the kitchen.

"Whoa, young lady. What's the hurry?" her Mom called out to her.

"I've gotta hurry up and eat, Mom. I've got lots to do," exclaimed Jenny.

"Well, I'm glad to see you so excited this morning. Do you have time for your breakfast, or are you in too big a hurry to eat your funny, sunny eggs this morning?" she asked with a snicker.

"Yes, I have to eat. I have a lot to do and I need my breakfast for energy," she smiled. She downed the eggs without hardly chewing. She picked up the bacon and nibbled quickly.

Mom looked at Jenny with a puzzled look on her face, "What is it that's so important this morning, Jenny? Do you have special plans?" She was afraid Jenny wanted to go see Jericho and they weren't allowing any visitors yet. Jericho's mom had called earlier that morning and said he was still not awake, but the doctors were saying he was out of danger now.

"Jenny, Jericho's mom called this morning and said he couldn't have visitors yet."

"Don't worry Mom. Jericho is going to be okay. The angels told me so," Jenny exclaimed happily.

"The angels?" asked her mother.

"Yeah. They said he was just sleeping until his head got better and then he would wake up."

She smiled at Jenny's confidence and turned back to finish washing the pans from breakfast. She looked back at Jenny again and Jenny was nearly finished eating.

"Mom?" asked Jenny.

"Yes dear?" answered her mother.

"Is the boy that was driving the car in the hospital with Jericho?"

Her mom looked at her and said very cautiously, "Yes. He is. His name is Evan and he's very, very sick. They really don't know if he'll be okay or not."

"I know," said Jenny, "I have to help him hear his angel and then he'll be okay."

"I don't know Jenny," said her mother, "Maybe you'd better not go to the hospital today. He's very sick and they probably won't let you see him anyway."

"I have to go, Mom," said Jenny, "I promised the angels."

Her mother could hear the commitment and determination in her daughter's voice. She knew she had to help her do whatever it was she felt she had to do,

"Okay, baby. We'll go to the hospital after we get cleaned up, but remember, he's very sick and you may not be able to see him or Jericho today."

Jenny jumped up from the table, ran over to hug her mom, and ran back upstairs to get ready. Her mother smiled as she watched her running up the stairs. She was such a good little girl. She stopped and thanked God for such a loving and caring daughter. She was truly blessed.

Jenny hoped the angels were with her now and could help her get in to talk to Evan. She would need everyone's help and she was so glad her mother seemed to understand. She almost always did.

Chapter Four
THE FIRST VISIT

On the way to the hospital Jenny's mother could see her excitement changing to concern.

"What could she be thinking?" wondered her mother. She looks like she has the weight of the world on her shoulders.

"You okay baby?" asked her mother.

"Yeah. I'm just asking the angels for help. If I can hear them and they are always with us, then they should be able to hear me, right?"

"I suppose so," said her mother.

"Kinda like saying my prayers, right?" asked Jenny again.

"I suppose so," answered her mother, "I know God always hears us, especially when we pray. Just exactly what did these little angels ask you to do?"

Jenny thought a minute and then began to tell her mother about her dream. Her mother watched her face as she told the story and watched the peaceful calm that came over Jenny as she talked about God's little angels and Heaven's Gate. She was so touched she could feel the warmth that came from Jenny and she began to share in Jenny's determination.

They pulled up to a parking space just outside the hospital doors. Jenny calmly got out of the car and looked up at the 20-story building. "Sure is big, isn't it?" said Jenny.

"Yes it is," replied her mother, "You were born right up there on the fourth floor. That was one of the happiest days of my life."

"Do you know where Jericho and Evan are?" she asked.

"Yes. Evan is in the Critical Care Unit on the third floor and Jericho has been moved to the second floor. He is out of danger, so they put him on the floor with the other children," said her mother.

"Let's go see Jericho first," said Jenny. She walked very slowly through the doors of the hospital, and seemed to be praying with every step. Her mother took her hand and looked down at her and smiled.

"What a little angel," her mom thought to herself.

They got off the elevator on the second floor and walked up to a big desk where all the nurses seemed to be coming and going from. It looked to Jenny like a beehive.

Her mom stopped one of the nurses and asked, "Can you tell me where Jericho Saunders is?"

"Yes. He's in room 204, but the doctor is in with him and his parents right now. Just go around the corner and wait outside the room. They'll be out once the doctor is through examining him," the nurse replied.

"Thank you," Jenny and her mom responded at the same time.

They smiled at the nurse and turned down the hall. Jenny was looking at the numbers on the doors and began to smile. She looked up at her mom and squeezed her hand.

When they got to room 204, there was a sign on the door that said, "No Visitors". They stood outside the door and watched the nurses coming and going from the different rooms. There were children in the halls, children in the waiting room with family and children in the nurses' station. They were everywhere. It was just like Heaven's Gate, except these little angels were sick.

Jenny began to get nervous again and then remembered God's little angels, "He's just asleep. He'll wake up when his head gets better," they had said.

The door to the room opened and out stepped a big man in a white jacket. "Hello," he said. He looked down at Jenny and smiled. "I'm Dr. Jeffrey. You must be waiting to see Jericho."

"Yes," said Jenny very timidly, "He's my best friend. The angels said he would be okay. Is he awake yet?"

The doctor looked at Jenny and her mom and quickly reached over to the door and took off the "No Visitors" sign. He turned to Jenny's mom and said, "Please take her in. This little one could make anyone well again," He turned to Jenny and said, "He's still sleeping, but he should wake up soon."

Jenny slowly pushed the door open and walked softly inside the room. Jericho's mom was holding his hand and talking across the bed to Jericho's father. She looked very concerned and his dad wasn't saying anything at all. He just stood and looked at Jericho with tears in his eyes.

Jenny walked over to Jericho's mom and took her hand. She looked up at Mrs. Saunders and smiled, "He'll be okay. The angels told me so. He's just sleeping."

Mrs. Saunders squeezed her hand and smiled down at her, "Bless you child. You are an angel," she whispered.

Jenny's mom went over and hugged Mrs. Saunders and Jenny leaned over and whispered into Jericho's ear, "You gotta sleep now Jericho so your head will get better. School starts next week and we get to see all of our friends again."

After Jenny's mom talked to Mrs. Saunders a few minutes and tried to console Mr. Saunders, Jenny tugged on her sleeve and announced it was time to go. Mrs. Saunders gave Jenny a hug and smiled, thanking them both for their kindness. Mr. Saunders just stood in the window, glancing back at his son waiting for him to wake up.

Once they were out in the hall Mom told Jenny that the police had been there to talk to Mrs. Saunders about Evan. Evan was in a lot of trouble, but still was not able to talk to anyone. Jenny began to pray silently again and ask for help.

They took the elevator and got off on the third floor. The sign said, "Pediatric Critical Care". They went to another big desk where the nurses were and Jenny's mom asked one of the nurses where Evan Douglas was. The nurse just looked at the two of them and pointed down the hall, "Last room on the left, but no visitors. He's in bad shape. Probably won't make it." The nurse turned and left.

Jenny looked at Mom and smiled again and said, "Come on Mom. I have to go see him."

They walked slowly down the hall. Each room had windows from the hallway into the room, but most had curtains pulled together so you couldn't see in. In the rooms with the curtains open, you could see children with machines all around. Some had blinking lights and there were all kinds of noises coming from these machines. It was very quiet and there were people standing outside the windows talking to doctors or just standing and looking in at the children.

When they got to Evan's room there were two police officers talking to a boy on crutches and two adults. Jenny's mom tugged at her hand to stop,

"You wait here dear and let me go see what's going on. We may need to wait and come back later."

Jenny just stood and watched as her mother walked over to the group standing in front of Evan's window. The police officer looked back at Jenny and then the other two adults nodded to Jenny's mom. The boy just watched Evan lying in bed. He never said a word.

Mom came back towards Jenny and reached for her hand, "We can't go in, but Evan's parents and these police officers would like to meet you."

Jenny looked up at Mom and tried to smile, but she was suddenly very scared. "Think of the angels," Jenny thought, "They are with you and you don't have to be afraid."

As they got to the window Jenny saw Evan laying in bed. The top of his head was wrapped in white strips of cloth and his neck was in a brace. There was a long tube going from a machine into his mouth and long skinny tubes going from bags to his arms. He didn't look like he was breathing at all, but the machines were blinking and one machine looked like it had a pump in it going up and down.

The police officers were still talking to Evan's parents. The police officers were asking why Evan was driving the car. His parents were very angry and not really saying much.

"We have done everything we know to do with this boy. You don't understand. He stays in trouble no matter what we do," said the woman.

The man was so mad you could see the veins throbbing in his neck and his face was very red.

"I think we're just lucky he didn't kill anybody. What an idiot! Don't these kids think about anything but having a good time? What if the little boy dies? Will we be held responsible?"

"Poor Evan," Jenny thought, "Maybe he better not wake up."

The couple looked down at Jenny, afraid that she had come to blame them for her friend being hurt. They were so angry they couldn't see the love and concern in Jenny's face as she looked at Evan. Jenny whispered to the couple, "Has he been asleep the whole time?"

"Yes," said the woman, "He moans from time to time, but hasn't really said anything yet."

Jenny took Mrs. Douglas' hand just like she had taken Mrs. Saunders' hand and said, "Jericho is sleeping too, but just until his head gets better. Then he'll wake up."

"So, you think everything is gonna be okay," the woman mocked, "What makes you so sure?"

"God's angels told me that Jericho would be okay, but Evan has to learn to hear his angel's voice before he will be okay. Benjamin has so much to say to him. He can help Evan if Evan will only hear him talking to him. They've sent me to teach him how," Jenny said very nervously.

The woman looked into Jenny's eyes and then looked at her son. "Angels?" the woman asked, "Why would angels care anything about Evan?"

Jenny just squeezed her hand tighter and smiled. She looked at Evan lying in the bed and began to talk silently to the angels, "What can I do? I can't go in there and he's so sick. He can't possibly be helped this way."

Just then Evan opened his eyes and slowly turned his head towards the window. Mrs. Douglas looked at Jenny and squeezed her hand as if she knew Jenny had something to do with Evan waking up.

"Get the doctor," she said calmly, "Evan is waking up."

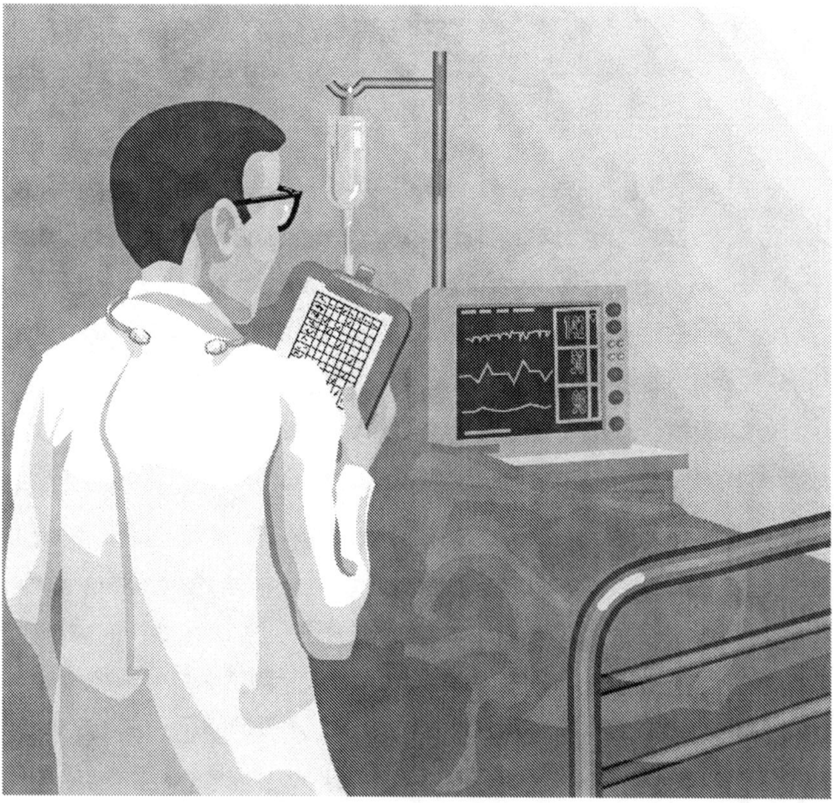

Chapter Five
MAKING FRIENDS

Jenny continued to visit with Jericho every day. They wouldn't let her stay long, but she did get to go in and talk for a few minutes every morning. It seemed to help his mom and dad to see Jenny every morning too. She just kept reminding them what the angels had told her. She would hug them both goodbye and then make her way to Evan's room.

This was her fourth trip to see Evan and she had only been allowed to stand at the window and watch him. His parents would be in the room and would come out when she would come up to the window. Mr. Douglas still looked angry, but Mrs. Douglas had started to look forward to seeing Jenny each morning. She smiled at Jenny today and gave her a hug.

"It's nice to see you again, Jenny," she said, "We've been telling Evan about you, but he hasn't said much. The doctor's say he's still in a bit of shock and trying to remember everything that has happened."

She kneeled down beside Jenny and looked into her eyes. "I've asked if you can come in and talk to Evan. They said it would be okay for a few minutes. Would you like to come in?"

Jenny thought for a moment and then nodded. Mrs. Douglas took her hand and led her inside the room to Evan's bed.

"Evan, this is Jenny. She's the little girl we've been telling you about."

Evan just stared at the ceiling. He gave no response. Jenny walked over to the side of Evan's bed and took his hand.

"Hi Evan. I'm glad you're getting better. Can you hear me Evan?"

Evan gave no response. He just continued to stare at the ceiling. He barely even blinked his eyes.

Jenny looked at Mrs. Douglas and managed a slight smile. Mrs. Douglas nodded to her to go ahead.

"Jericho is feeling better, but he's still sleeping. How are you feeling?" Jenny softly asked.

Still, there was no response from Evan.

Jenny just stood and looked at Evan for a minute and then said, "It's okay Evan. Sometimes I don't feel like talking either. You can just lay there and try to get better. Can you hear me Evan? If you can, just squeeze my hand."

Nothing happened. Jenny couldn't figure out what to do next. She didn't seem to be making any progress. Just then she looked at Evan and a tiny tear was sliding down his cheek. She reached over and wiped the tear away. Evan gently squeezed her hand. She squeezed back. She looked over at Evan's mother and gave a little smile. Evan's mother was brushing away her tears. Evan's father left the room.

"Evan. Jericho is going to be okay. He's just sleeping. Don't worry about him. I'm worried about you," Jenny said very kindly.

Evan just stared at the ceiling. Jenny couldn't figure out what to say now, so she just held Evan's hand. She didn't have much time. She just had to figure out a way to get through to Evan.

The next day Jenny's mom had to go help a friend with some things, and Jenny had to wait to go to the hospital until the afternoon. She was very upset that they didn't get to go at the usual time. She really had to get to see Evan. Her mom had promised they would go that afternoon, but the hours passed very slowly until she finally got home. Once her mom got home she was very tired and had laid down on the couch to rest.

"Jenny, would it be okay if we didn't go to the hospital today? Mom is really tired."

"Oh please, Mom. We have to go. I know you're tired, but Evan needs me and he still can't hear Benjamin's voice."

Mom looked at Jenny and even though she was exhausted, something told her she had to do this for Jenny. She got up, took Jenny's hand and said, "Come on baby. Let's go get Evan to hear Benjamin talking to him."

Jenny was very excited. She almost ran to the car, pulling Mom behind her.

When they got to the hospital, the doctors had just made their rounds. Jericho was doing much better, but was still not awake. Evan was still about the same, and just staring at the ceiling. Mrs. Douglas said he just wouldn't respond to anyone but Jenny.

Jenny went over to Evan and said, "Hi Evan. How ya feeling today?"

Evan turned and looked at Jenny for the first time. He started to smile, but then tears started to fill his eyes again. Jenny looked at him and smiled and said, "Look, we have a lot of work to do. You've got to get better so we can teach you to hear Benjamin's voice."

Evan looked very confused. He struggled to speak, "I thought the kid's name was Jericho."

"Jericho is my best friend. Benjamin is your angel's name," announced Jenny.

Everyone was smiling and beginning to relax. He was finally talking and though it was only a few words, he was at least responding.

"I don't know any Benjamin," Evan struggled to speak. "Does he go to Westerman High?"

"No, silly. He doesn't go to school. He's an angel," giggled Jenny.

Evan just rolled his eyes, "An angel, huh?"

"You're makin' this awful tough Evan, and you're gonna' keep him from flying if you're not careful."

Jenny was getting pretty put out by this boy. She was not going to be teased by Evan, and was about to turn and march right out of the room when she saw her reflection in the window and remembered Laurel, Mica and Benjamin. They were counting on her and God wanted her to keep trying.

"I'm sorry about your friend, kid," said Evan, "I didn't see him and couldn't stop. I just knew I had killed him."

"I already told you. Don't worry about him. He'll be okay. Our angels were looking out for us," she said rather indignantly.

"Yeah? Well where was my angel while all this was going on?" asked Evan, "or do they only help little kids?"

"Your angel was with you too," she snapped back at him, "and he got hurt trying to make you listen. Now he may never fly again and he's got a broken wing?"

Jenny started crying. She was really getting frustrated. His attitude didn't show that he believed in

God, in angels, or anything else. He sure wasn't going to hear one talking to him.

Jenny's mom came over and put her hand on Jenny's shoulder, "Jenny," she said very calmly, "have faith little one. If you don't have the faith to believe that God knows the way to reach Evan, then how can Evan have the faith to believe what you're telling him is true?"

Jenny looked up at her mom and smiled again. She wiped away the tears with determination and said, "Look you. I know I'm just a little kid, but haven't you ever believed in God? Haven't you ever wondered who kept you safe when you were in trouble? Haven't you ever heard something or someone telling you in the back of your mind that you'd better behave?"

The boy looked at Jenny and Jenny continued on until she was exhausted. It was time to go and she felt she hadn't made any progress. What was she going to do?

"Are you coming back tomorrow?" Evan asked hopefully.

Jenny turned to him and smiled. She ran back over to the bed and gave him a gentle hug.

"Yes," she said softly, "If I give up now, you'll never see Heaven's Gate and Benjamin will never fly. That would be a real shame."

Evan looked puzzled, "Heaven's Gate?" he thought.

That night Jenny asked her mom what else she could possibly do, "I've told him about the angels and he just laughed at me," she said, "What am I going to do?"

"Jenny, sometimes we think we're too old to learn anything from the children around us. We just think we know it all already. You have to keep trying sweetheart. If this is something you truly believe in and have faith, you will be able to help him, but you have to have faith. Why don't you ask God to send some help when you say your prayers tonight and see what He comes up with."

Jenny loved her mother dearly. She was so kind and loving. Jenny thought, "Maybe if Evan's parents had been more like Mom, he would be able to hear his angel too."

Jenny went upstairs and brushed her teeth. She pulled the covers back on her bed and looked out the window. She could see the stars in the sky and wondered if the little angels were starting to gather at Heaven's Gate.

She went to the window and sat on the bench under the window. She leaned her head over against the window seal and watched the moon lazily pass through the clouds. She walked over to her bed, pulled off her robe and laid it across the end of her bed, crawled underneath the covers and began her bedtime prayer. As she was finishing her prayers she asked God for help and drifted off to sleep.

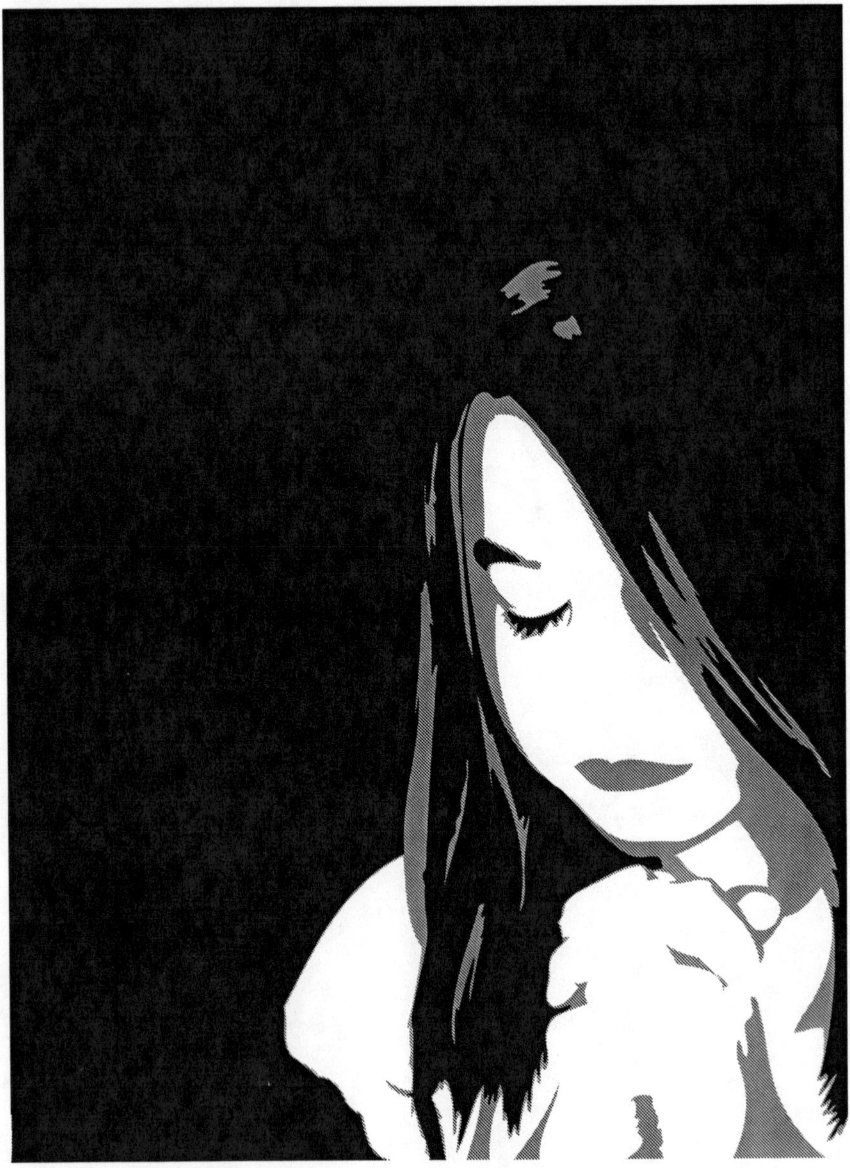

Chapter Six
THE PLAN

"Jenny ... Jenny ...", she recognized the voice immediately, "Wake up. We don't have much time."

"Laurel!" cheered Jenny, "I'm so glad to see you."

"We've been with you all along Jenny. You're doing fine. Just be his friend and he'll want to know what you know. Then, you can teach him to listen," said Laurel in an understanding tone.

"But I don't think he believes in angels, Laurel. He makes fun of me when I talk about you."

"He believed at one time," said Laurel, "and he can believe again."

"When did he believe?" asked Jenny, "Why did he stop believing?"

"It was when he was a little older than you that he began to stop believing. His family has had a lot of problems and his parents weren't home very much. They fought a lot and it didn't seem to Evan that he could do anything right. No matter how hard he tried. It just didn't seem to him like there could possibly be anyone who cared about him anymore and he just quit believing in anything, especially in God, and of course in angels."

Jenny looked around at the angels again and wished she could stay longer. It was so peaceful and tranquil here. The air was filled with love and hope. Then she had an idea.

"What if I could prove to him there were angels? Maybe then he would be able to hear Benjamin. He has to believe again."

Laurel sat and studied the problem. "How to prove there are angels," she thought. Laurel looked at Jenny and said, "Okay, this is your only chance. Remind him about the time he went into the old warehouse on Rustleman Docks and about the pack of cigarettes he took from his dad's jacket pocket. Ask him if he got scared when he heard someone talking to him, telling him he was gonna get caught and he should go back home. He was so scared he threw the cigarettes in the river, and he ran back home and crawled under the bed. He hasn't touched a cigarette since. There was nobody there with him that could have told you this story and he listened to the voices rather than do something wrong. By that time it took fear to make him listen. He had already stopped listening to Benjamin by that time, and seldom listened again after that."

"This might work," said Jenny, "It has to."

Again, Jenny said her goodbyes. Laurel gave her the special kiss on the cheek and she began to drift off to sleep once again.

"He has to believe now," Jenny thought.

Jenny woke up feeling refreshed and encouraged. She ran downstairs to tell Mom about the plan. Mom smiled and said, "See. Just take your problems to the Lord, and the solutions will come. Let's hurry up and eat so we can get you to the hospital to see Jericho and Evan."

As usual, Jenny stopped by Jericho's room first and visited with his family. He had been asleep for days now and school was starting in three days.

"I think we may have a good plan now Jericho. Don't you worry. You'll be awake soon," Jenny whispered to Jericho.

She gave Mrs. Saunders a hug and turned to go confront Evan. He just had to listen now.

When Jenny arrived at Evan's room, Evan's mom was crying. She looked at Jenny's mom and cried, "He's gone into a coma. They don't think he's going to make it."

"Can I go in?" Jenny asked.

"I'll take you in dear. They really don't want him to have any visitors, but we'll hurry and sneak you in."

She took Jenny's hand and led her through the door to Evan's bed. Jenny took Evan's hand in hers and stroked it gently.

"Evan, don't give up. I talked to the angels again last night. I know you don't believe in angels anymore, but you used to. You used to hear Benjamin's voice. He used to be able to keep you out of trouble. Then you quit believing. Try to remember Evan. Just try. If you can just believe again, then you can hear his voice."

She continued to stroke his hand gently and talk very softly, "Do you remember the time you took your dad's cigarettes from his jacket pocket. Remember that you went to Rustleman Docks and snuck into the old warehouse to smoke the cigarettes. Don't you remember the voice you heard, Evan? It was Benjamin talking to you. They had to scare you for you to listen anymore." He was not responding to her at all and she was beginning to get very scared. She was loosing him and she didn't know what to do.

His mother just stood and watched. Jenny's mom stood outside the room looking in through the window and praying.

"Remember, you got so scared when you heard the voice that you threw the cigarettes in the river and ran all the way home," Jenny leaned over to Evan and gave him a gentle kiss on the cheek, a special kiss. "Remember your angel's voice?" she whispered in his ear. "Dear God, please help Evan."

Jenny stood back up and looked at Evan's face. He looked at her and smiled, "Hi Jen," he said softly. "Benjamin said to tell you hello."

Everyone was so excited. He was awake and the doctor's couldn't believe his recovery. Jenny was so happy she cried and her mom beamed with pride. Evan's mom was very glad for a second chance to love her son. In all the celebrating it was very difficult to hear the voice coming from the hall.

"Jenny!" cried Jericho, "Mica, says hi!"

Jenny had never been so happy. She had her friend back, Evan was going to be okay and Benjamin was gonna fly again.

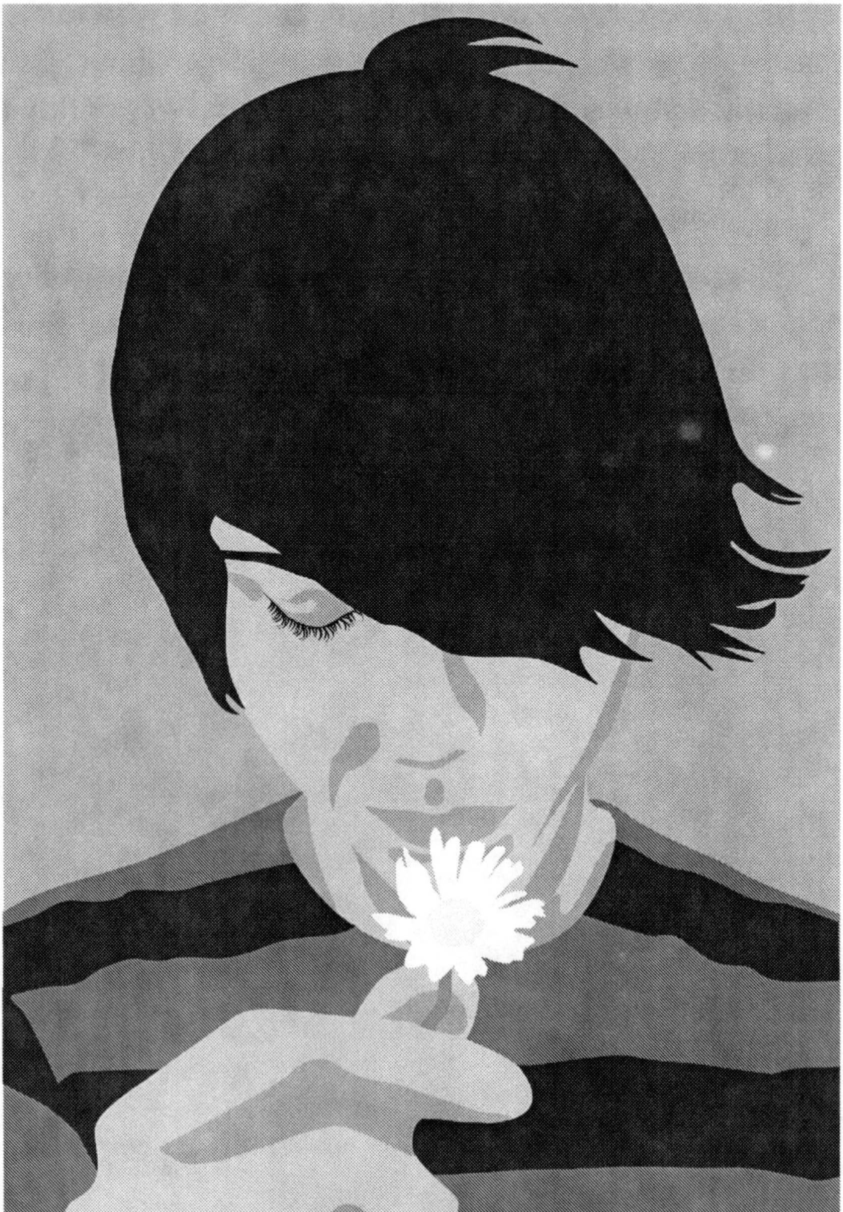

Chapter Seven

AN EXTRA SEAT ON THE BUS

Jenny had continued to go visit Evan in the hospital. He had a lot of work to do before he could get out of the hospital. He was going to be there for a while. His mother had decided that the family needed some help and his father had agreed to try listening and spend some time with Evan. They all decided it was about time to find a Church. After all, <u>God</u> had sent them Jenny. It was time they did something for <u>God</u>.

Evan really looked forward to Jenny visiting and began to talk to Jenny about things he should have done differently. He and

Jericho became friends too and it helped Evan a lot to know he hadn't hit Jericho with the car.

Jenny and Jericho started making plans for school again and talked about finally getting to see all their friends. They only had one more day. Their moms took them shopping the day before school started to get some school supplies and new clothes. They talked together about God and angels and friends, and how blessed they all were to be together.

They went to bed early that night and each said their special prayers for Evan and all the other kids who were having trouble hearing their angels. They said a special prayer for all the angels at Heaven's Gate and wondered how many other children had been lucky enough to see it. They vowed to never forget and to share the stories with anyone who would listen. It was difficult to sleep and the morning seemed like it would never come.

Finally, the day had arrived. The minutes seemed like hours to Jenny and Jericho.

They sped through their breakfast and grabbed their book bags. They pulled their moms down the sidewalk to the bus stop.

It was so exciting to see the bus pull up to the bus stop. It was big and yellow and all the kids were waving and excited about the first day of school. Jenny grabbed Jericho's hand and said, "Come on Jericho. We gotta go start school today."

The mothers just stood together watching their children grow up right before their very eyes.

"Okay," Jericho said and hurried along with Jenny.

Just as Jenny turned and looked back at Jericho there were Mica and Laurel following right behind. She turned to Jericho and said, "We'd better save an extra seat."

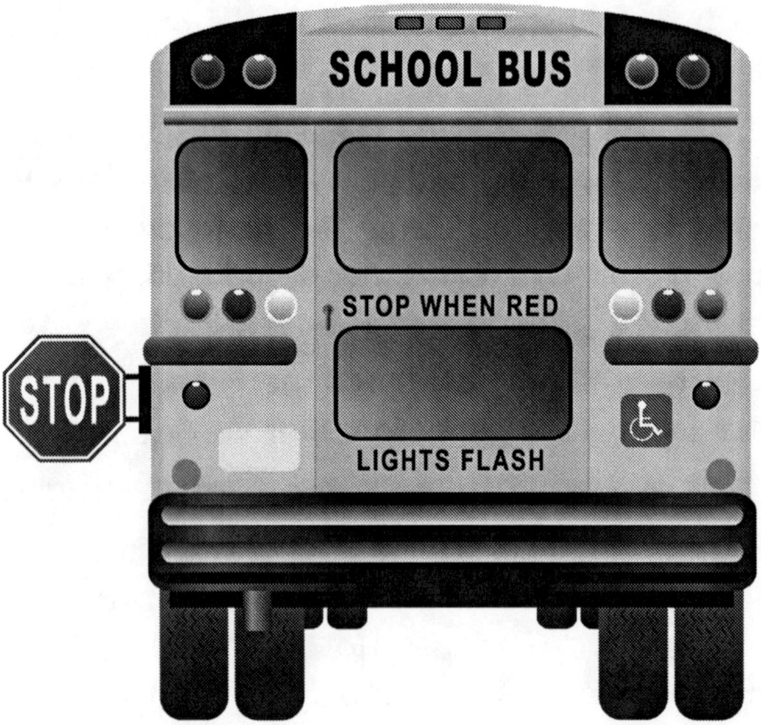
SCHOOL BUS
STOP WHEN RED
LIGHTS FLASH
STOP